Two Hundred Rabbits

Lonzo Anderson and Adrienne Adams

THE VIKING PRESS

NEW YORK

 First published in 1968 by The Viking Press, Inc., 625 Madison Avenue, New York, N.Y. 10022. Published simultaneously in Canada by The Macmillan Company of Canada Limited. Library of Congress catalog card number: 68-16067.

Printed in U.S.A. by Reehl Litho, Inc.

Pic Bk

For Anne MacKenzie Wyneken
and her children's children's children . . .

In my travels I came to the land of Jamais and stopped on a hill to look at the valley below.

A forest was in the middle of the view, and on one side of it stood the king's castle, surrounded by a moat full of water.

On the other side of the forest was a cottage made of stone and wood, with straw for a roof.

Someone was working in the garden near the cottage.

I love vegetables, especially lettuce, so I went down for a closer look.

The someone was a young boy. He whistled and sang as he worked.

His garden was the neatest and prettiest I had ever seen.

"Hmm," I said to myself. "This boy is really special. Great things are going to happen to him."

I decided to stop here in my travels for a while. It would be fun, as long as I could keep out of sight and just watch.

The garden had a good fence around it, so I stayed outside; but when the boy cleaned out his lettuce bed he threw over enough lettuce to fill me up, and after dark I ate it.

Early the next morning the boy set out through the forest toward the king's castle, carrying his lunch. I hustled along, keeping near him without his noticing me.

When he came out of the forest it was hard for me to follow him without being seen; but if he had looked around at me, I could have pretended to be on my way somewhere else.

The boy came to the castle moat. The guard stopped him at the drawbridge.

"What do you want?" he demanded.

"Isn't this the Festival Day at the castle?"

"It is," the guard replied, stiff as his staff.

"I wish to entertain the king," the boy said, "and maybe he will give me a steady job."

"Oh?" The guard raised an eyebrow. "And what can you do to entertain the king?"

"I can stand on my head longer than almost anybody."

"The king would not be amused," the guard said.

"I can skate faster than . . ."

"In *summer*?" The guard raised his other eyebrow.

"I can swim . . ."

The guard was shaking his head.

"Then what *do* people do to entertain the king?" the boy asked.

"Some sing," the guard said.

The boy went into the forest to practice singing. He sang, and the birds all flew out of the forest in horror. Even I felt like stopping up my ears.

"Oh, this will never do!" I said to myself. "If only he could think of something better!"

The boy went again to the guard and asked, "What else do people do to entertain the king?"

"Some play musical instruments," the guard said.

The boy ran home for his fiddle and went into the forest to practice playing. The squirrels and chipmunks and foxes and wolves all came to scold him, but I kept as quiet as I could. I was still panting from running to keep up with him.

"Oh, this is not good," I said to myself. I could hear the sounds of the festival at the castle. "If only he could think of a fine idea before it is too late!"

The boy took his fiddle home, then scampered once more to the guard.

"What else do people do?" he asked, out of breath.

"Some juggle," the guard said.

The festival was almost half over. The boy did not stop to listen to the happy roar in the courtyard. He hurried into the forest to practice juggling.

He juggled with sticks and stones and old pine cones, but they all slipped through his hands or fell on his head. The birds and animals watched him and sneered and jeered.

He sat down on a log. My heart ached for him, he looked so discouraged. Soon the festival would be over, and he would have lost his chance to entertain the king.

Suddenly, an old woman was standing there.

The boy jumped up and bowed.

"You look sad," the old woman said.

He smiled. "I didn't mean to," he said. "Won't you sit down and rest?"

"Thank you, I think I will," the old woman said.

They sat together on the log.

"You do have troubles, though," she said.

He sighed. "Life is more difficult than I ever thought, when it comes to making my way in the world."

"Tell me about it," she said.

As he told her, he shared his sausages with her. He gave her more than half. I could see his eyes as he looked at her thin, old face; he thought she was starving.

"But," she said when he had finished his story, "the best way to catch the king's attention is to show him something that no one else has in all the world."

"Yes," the boy said, "but what?"

"Do you know how to make a slippery-elm slide whistle?" the old woman asked.

"Why, yes," he said. "Doesn't everyone?"

"Let me see you do it," she said.

He found a slippery-elm tree. It had many twigs of the right size and smoothness for a whistle, but one in particular wriggled, as if to catch his eye, while all the others kept still.

He cut the enchanted twig with his sheath knife and made it the right length.

The old woman was watching him like a hawk. She nodded approvingly as he cut and notched and sliced and tapped until it was finished.

"What a clever boy!" I said to myself. Never had I seen a whistle like this.

“Blow it,” the old woman said.

He blew, and by sliding the lower part of the twig up and down inside the slippery bark as he blew into the mouthpiece, he was able to play a tune.

At the sound all the rabbits that lived in the forest came running, and crowded about him.

“A magic whistle!” the boy cried, and I danced for joy.

“Blow it again,” the old woman said.

He blew, and the rabbits lined up like soldiers.

There were twenty rows of them, ten in each row but the last. In the last row there were only nine.

“Tch-tch!” the old woman said. “How annoying. A hundred and ninety-nine rabbits. They don’t come out even. I’m sorry.”

"But what does it matter? This is wonderful!"

The boy looked at the rabbits, and they looked at him as if they were ready to follow him anywhere.

"Atten-*tion*!" he cried.

The rabbits stood straight up, like soldiers.

"Forward, *march*!"

The rabbits marched through the forest toward the king's castle, the boy leading them with short steps so as not to leave them behind. He played a bouncy little tune on his whistle, nodding and bowing his thanks to the old woman.

I was so excited I was shivering. What a wonderful thing it was, that rabbit parade! But oh, was it too late for the festival? How I hoped the boy would be in time!

Out of the forest the rabbits went marching. They were having such fun I was tempted to march with them. But I was a stranger there, and the old woman's magic was not for me.

The festival was not over yet. Some people were coming out of the courtyard, but others were going in.

The king looked out of his window and saw the marvelous marching rabbits. He called to invite them to cross the drawbridge, and they did. And so did I, losing myself in the crowd.

The king came down from his room and sat on his courtyard throne to review the parade.

In the excitement I crawled under the throne from behind, to keep out of the way and have a good view.

"Halt!" the king shouted suddenly.

The boy stopped the parade and the marching tune.

"That last row!" the king said crossly. "It doesn't come out even!"

"True, Your Majesty," the boy said, bowing.

"Well, it looks silly," the king complained. "It looks ragged. *Away with those last nine rabbits!*"

"But, Your Majesty," the boy said, "that would break their hearts!"

"Hmph," the king said. "I suppose it would. Hmmm . . . *Then get another rabbit!*"

"But Your Majesty," the boy said, "there is not one other rabbit in our whole forest."

"Oh," His Majesty said, scowling. He cocked his head and thought, while I held my breath, waiting.

Then, *"Away with all of you!"* he roared.

Now I had no choice. How could I just sit there and not help?

I popped out from under the king's throne and took my place in the last row of rabbits.

That made everything all right.

The boy smiled. He took up his tune where he had left off, and gave the signal to march. We paraded in front of the king, who clapped his hands and cried:

"This will make my court the most popular court in the whole world!"

Oh, well. I was tired of traveling anyway.

BOUND
HUNTTING